I0699780

Working Blue Press

First Edition

ISBN 978-1-967038-18-3 (Kindle)
ISBN 978-1-967038-19-0 (Print)

For all the men and women who love
great sex, great relationships, and a
damn good time.

Content

Suggestions for Further Reading

Men Who Renovate Erotic Series
Books 1, 2, 3 and 4.

Follow Lacey Love on Amazon to keep abreast of new releases!

April
Showers

Men Who Renovate Erotic Series

Book 4

April Showers

Ben wasn't entirely proud of what had transpired with April Jay over the spring, but he also wasn't mad about it, either.

"The spoiled one you bitched about endlessly?" Wolfe asked. He leaned back in his metal chair, shoving the last of his donut in his mouth and swallowing. "That's who you're…wait, what are you doing with her?"

"Yeah, I thought you couldn't stand her? The selfie girl, right?" Jack asked. He took a sip of his coffee, then ran his hand through his black hair and grinned.

"Didn't you say she was like a Valley Girl crossed with a Kardashian, then multiplied times, like, one thousand?" Danny asked. His dark eyes were filled with humor.

The three men laughed as they stared at Ben.

"So not your type," Wolfe said. He shook his head, his dark hair short and spiky.

"She's not," Ben said defensively. At least, she hadn't ever been his type. Ben was a serious man, who had joined the Army Reserves for four years after college and just got out last year. He liked routines, covert operations, and serious girls.

April was none of those things.

"You know what, let's talk about you for a second," Ben said, trying to avert attention from himself. "So, you and Gina broke up?"

Wolfe shifted in his chair with a sigh. His icy blue eyes taking on a disappointed glint. "We did."

"You're welcome to stay at my place as long as you need to, man," Danny said.

"Thanks," Wolfe said. "I'm checking out a new place at that apartment complex you did."

Danny and Wolfe smiled broadly at each other.

"Maybe Jenny and her friends are back," Wolfe quipped.

"No way, man, Jenny is off-limits," Danny said. "But her friends, yeah, maybe they're around."

"Well, you can find out right?" Jack asked. "Haven't you and Jenny been texting?"

Danny smiled. "That's a story for a different day," he said. "How's Ariel?"

The four of them were masterful at changing topics to avoid talking. Ben grinned. It kept the attention of him as Jack's green eyes lit up.

"She's….damn, she's amazing," he said. Ben hadn't ever seen Jack like this. Jack had been the player in college and then dealt with his mother's death. Having a serious girlfriend had never been his thing—until Ariel.

"We're, uh, we're talking about moving in together," Jack said.

"No shit?" Wolfe exclaimed. "That's awesome."

"What's it been? Like three, four months?" Danny asked.

Jack nodded. "Yep. Met the parents. The brothers and sisters. The whole thing."

"Congrats, man," Ben offered. "Ariel's awesome. Good for you guys."

They all turned back to him. Shit.

"Yeah, now, back to you, master of avoidance," Wolfe said. And now Ben was facing three stares that weren't going to let him out of this office without spilling his story about April.

"Alright." Ben sighed. "So, here's what happened."

2

Ben the Help

Ben walked up to the front door of the small condo on the West side of Cleveland in the Lakewood area. Rich people area was what he called it. And this condo was in a rich complex for young adults who had Daddy's money to spend. The HOA fee alone was almost one grand a month.

"It's open!" The female voice was young, rude, and demanding—everything he didn't like in any person, male or female.

He rolled his eyes and took a sharp inhale of air, then did a slow exhale. "Be nice, be nice, be nice," he whispered.

He grabbed the handle and pushed, opening the door into a

lush cream and natural decorated
living room with high-end furniture
and gorgeous natural light. If he
had the money, it's exactly what he
would do with the place. A rush of
footsteps turned his attention to the
kitchen area, where marble
counters and floors shined against
the stainless-steel appliances and
white cupboards. Stunning.

And so was she. He felt the
breath escape his throat before he
could do anything about it.

"You're the help?" she asked.
Her cute nose scrunched up as she
leveled her bright blue eyes at him.
Her skin was perfectly tanned, and
her face was a masterpiece even AI
couldn't create no matter how
many prompts it was given.

"Uh," he said. Nice. He needed
to say actual words.

"The help?" he snarked.

Of all the things he could have
said, like, "Wow, you're fucking

gorgeous," or "Hi, I'm your next boyfriend," it was his sudden annoyance at her calling him "the help" that came flying out.

"Well, you're renovating my shower, I'm not sure what else to call you."

"You could start with my na—"

"Bathroom's upstairs," she interrupted, cutting him off. She flipped her hair and turned back into the kitchen.

That. Bitch. He raised an eyebrow and gripped his toolbox as he started toward the staircase. He could hear her talking in the kitchen about a smoothie recipe, so he stopped at the bottom of the stairs and peered in to see what she was doing.

There was a selfie stand with her iPhone on it, lighting, and smoothie ingredients with a blender. She looked camera-ready, her breasts perky in a tight, pink tank top and short white shorts. Her long, espresso-colored hair tumbled down her back and chest in big, bouncy curls. No doubt he wanted his hands in those shiny strands as he kissed her, but he also felt a deep desire to tell her what a spoiled brat she was, too.

"Can I help you?" she snapped as she caught him glancing at her.

"Ben," he snapped back.

"What?"

"My name," he said sarcastically. "It's Ben."

"Okay, Ben *the help*," she snarked. "Bathroom's upstairs. A week, right?"

"Yep," he said calmly. That was his military training kicking in. He'd had much worse drill sergeants screaming at him. He could take this dainty, little flower. "I'll be in and out for the next hour hauling in materials. Ma'am."

When she exhaled a sharp air at his use of Ma'am, he knew he'd found at least one thing to get on her nerves.

"I'm not a Ma'—"

"Later," he said interrupting her. He pretended to toss his hair over his shoulder before he sharply turned up the stairs. He shouldn't antagonize the client, but she really got under his skin.

"Ugh," she exclaimed from the kitchen. He laughed all the way to the top of the stairs, which was essentially a lofted master bedroom with a large bathroom. It was plush and clean.

Actually, it was military clean. The bed was perfectly made, everything was put in place, clothes perfectly hung in the walk-in closet, and shoes lined up neatly on their shelves.

"Huh," he whispered.

He turned into the bathroom and put down his toolbox. He made mental notes of where to lay down tarps, where to put things, materials, everything he needed to get this job done. He was excited to do the work. He loved using his hands and transforming spaces. When Wolfe had brought this idea to them, it was the perfect next thing for him to do while he figured out next steps.

The Army Reserves were a way to do some traveling, learn some new skills, and to honor his family. He came from a long line of military veterans who had served their country well. He wanted to do that, too. It was deeply engrained in him, and he was proud of his service. But now, it was time to figure out his life.

"I'm not paying you to stand around and do nothing," she said sharply.

He sucked in a deep breath. *Be nice, be nice, be nice.*

"*You* aren't paying me?" he sassed as he turned to face her, stepping within an inch of her. *Now see, that wasn't nice.*

Her icy stare made him grin. He'd found another thing to get under her skin.

"I don't care what you think you know about me," she snapped as she stepped to him. Her little nose was less than an inch from his lips. Holy shit, she smelled good. "I want this done in a week. So, hop to it. Ben the help."

She smirked at him and flipped her hair right in his face as she stormed out. He'd have been pissed but her hair smelled so damn good, and it was so soft, that he decided to forgive her for it. Sort of.

"Spoiled brat," he hissed under his breath. He peered out the door to watch her cute little figure stomp down the stairs. As if feeling his eyes on her, she glanced over her shoulder at him with a sultry little stare and disappeared back into the kitchen.

He grinned. "I'm gettin' to her."

He headed down the stairs himself and began the daunting task of unloading his truck and hauling everything upstairs. He took every opportunity he got to slam the door, stomp the stairs, and bang his tools. Anything to make enough noise to disrupt her video.

"Hello!" she yelled. "Working here."

He popped into the kitchen, the final box of tiles in his hands. By now, he was hot on this warm, spring day, and he'd removed his jacket. His tight, baby blue T-shirt showed off all the work he'd put in at the gym.

"I'm sorry, am I making too much noise?" he asked. He grinned as he noticed her eyes hungrily take in his well-built form and how good it looked in his T-shirt and jeans.

"Uh," she uttered.

"Yes?"

She shifted her weight and readjusted her stare, slitting her eyes at him. "I need something off that shelf."

She flicked her eyes up to the top of the cabinets, where there was a decorative bowl and nothing else.

"You need that bowl?" He raised an eyebrow at her that clearly was saying, "I call bullshit."

"Yeah, I do."

"For what?"

"What does it matter?" she asked huffily.

He grinned.

"You know what, never mind," she huffed. She went back to her smoothies, which hadn't changed much since he first got there.

He was definitely getting to her.
He tried to hide his smile but it was
hard as he walked into the kitchen
and put his box of tiles down on
one of the kitchen tools. He walked
over to the cabinets, reached up,
and grabbed the bowl. He turned to
her and saw she was trying not to
peek at him while he did it. He
liked that even more.

He walked up right in front of
her and handed her the bowl. She
took it as she peered up into his
eyes. It made him catch his breath.
Damn, she was beautiful. Those
eyes…there was something there.

"Here you go," he said quietly.

She slowly took the bowl, never
breaking eye contact with him.

"Thanks."

They stayed like that for a few
seconds too long until he finally
had to either break the stare or take
her in his arms and kiss her deeply.

"You're welcome." He turned and grabbed the box of tiles. As he walked back to the stairs, he glanced over his shoulder and was pleased to find she was still staring at him. He grinned and, try as she might, she couldn't stop from smiling back.

"April," she said quickly.

"Yeah, it's April," he said questioningly.

"No," she said. A sexy blush spread from her throat to her cheeks. "My name. It's April. Ben. The Help."

This time when she insulted him, she gave it with a dose of seduction. It made a shiver of pleasure run from his pelvis to his chest.

"Pretty," he said.

"Thanks."

"I meant the basket." He grinned as she laughed and shook her head.

As he walked up the staircase he
wondered if April showers really
did bring May flowers.

3

Little Yellow Bikini

April knew as soon as Ben walked into her condo that she wanted him. And then almost immediately she was annoyed by how much she wanted him.

Her father would never approve of a guy like Ben that was for sure. First of all, he was dark-skinned, dark hair, and dark eyes—maybe Italian or something? She wasn't quite sure. All her father would see was that he didn't have pale skin, light eyes, and light hair.

That and so many other reasons were why she'd worked so hard for her social media following. It paid her a six-figure annual salary that guaranteed her freedom at age twenty-two. And she needed to be free from her family, her family's money, and her dad's control.

She knew from the start that her father expected her to marry someone from that world. Some rich guy with low morals and high balance bank accounts. She wasn't interested in that. She was one of those poor saps who believed in Romeo and Juliet type love—that passion and sex and turmoil from the intense emotions that kind of relationship elicited.

She'd probably read too many steamy romance novels in her lifetime, to be honest. She should probably stop reading them. Except then beautiful Ben and his Adonis stature walked in and suddenly she saw before her the leading man from every steamy romance novel in her Kindle. And now, those same books were inspiring her to get her passions met from this gorgeous,

funny, no bullshit, sexy-as-hell
man. A real man.

Until he got all huffy and looked
at her like she was some spoiled,
rich girl. That wasn't entirely
untrue—she had been that girl.
Until she turned eighteen, became a
social media influencer, and paid
for her own college degree, this
condo, her car, and even for him to
be here renovating her bathroom.

So, it pissed her off when he
gave her shade without even
knowing her. And that meant she
had to annoy him. Except then he
was cute about it, and she had him
get that basket off the top of the
cabinet. The basket that was now
sitting on the table unused because
she didn't actually need it. She just
wanted him to be close to her.

And now he'd been there for two
days doing exactly what he was
supposed to be doing—working.

"Just my luck," she whispered. She'd hired a company that actually did the work. And well. He was good, too. Damn good. And he was very militant about it. He arrived exactly at seven in the morning, took his lunch break exactly at noon, and left exactly at five in the evening. His shoes were always clean, he didn't track anything into her home, and his lunch was always a carefully coordinated mix of fruits, vegetables, chips, and a sandwich.

She knew all that because she'd been spying on him every chance she got. She'd even gotten him to glance her way a few times. The sultry stares between them made her got to bed every night and rub her aching pussy. She would always come with his name on her lips. But now the pressure had mounted. She wanted him. And she was going to have him, damn it.

"What would Alexandra do?" she uttered. Alexandra was the lead in her most recent novel and she was quite a character. Bold, seductive, and always got exactly the kind of sex she wanted. And April was going to steal a page from Alexandra's playbook.

She quickly stripped down to her tiny, yellow bikini and checked her hair and make-up in the mirror. Long and flowing locks, check. Shiny lips, check. Heaving breasts, check.

"Yes." She took a deep breath to steady her nerves and walked into the bathroom. "How's it going?"

When he glanced over to her from the shower where he was replacing the hardware, she saw his face transform from work to pleasure. It was exactly what she was hoping for.

She walked further into the bathroom as he stood up and she

noticed how firm he was between his legs. She was suddenly wet and ready for him as she reached up and touched her bare abdomen, lingering there as his eyes watched her intently.

"Going fine," he said huskily.

"I was thinking of taking a swim."

He took in her ample breasts, lingering there until her nipples were hard, then moving to her fingers on her stomach, her tiny little strings on her hips, between her legs, and back to her eyes.

"Pool isn't open yet," he whispered.

His voice was so low and sexy she could barely contain herself. He was absolutely the sexiest man she'd ever seen.

"Oh," she said, feigning stupidity. "I didn't realize."

He grinned at her. "Don't you have social media stuff to do?"

Her face dropped as anger zipped through her body.

"You're an asshole." She turned to storm out of the bathroom but felt his strong hands on her waist, pulling her gently back to him.

"April, wait," he said. He stepped up behind her and held her close, his mouth at her ear. "I'm sorry. I was teasing."

"Well, don't," she said quietly. She glanced over her shoulder into his eyes, rich and dark as they bore into her.

Both of them were breathing harder than they should and she was suddenly aware of how hard his cock was against her back. What would Alexandra do, indeed.

Fuck it.

She quickly wrapped her hand in his hair and pulled him into a deep kiss as he moaned and turned her body around so he could press against her body. He walked her backwards to the bathroom wall and sunk his tongue deep in her mouth as he ravaged her with a passionate kiss.

His rough hand found its way under her bikini top, rubbing her nipple and squeezing her gently.

"Yes," she panted.

He quickly kissed down her throat and put one nipple in his mouth, then the other, sucking and licking her in a way no man ever had before.

"Ben," she moaned. "More."

He pulled off her top and then her bottoms, before kissing down her stomach and making his way to her wet slit.

"Yes!"

She felt his tongue slide into her pussy and swirl around her clit, sending pulses of pleasure through her body.

"Fuck," he moaned. "You taste so good, April."

Hearing her name on his lips caused a jolt of electricity to shoot through her.

"Yes, baby, yes," she said.

He slipped his fingers deep inside her, thrusting as he sucked her clit, the other hand sliding up to take her breast in his hand.

"Holy shit," she panted. "I'm gonna come, Ben. I'm gonna come!"

The explosion of pleasure inside her was almost too much for her to keep standing. She gripped his hair and pulsed her pussy against his face as the waves rocked her body.

She'd never experienced anything like that. Not with a man like him.

As her orgasm ebbed and her breathing returned to normal, she felt Ben lightly kissing her between the legs, on her inner thighs and her lower abs. He peered at her with big, dark eyes.

"Did you come good, baby?" he whispered.

She pulled on his hair as she grinned and nodded.

"Good," he said quietly. He grabbed her bikini and stood up, handing them to her. "You're beautiful."

She took them and smiled. "Thank you."

She wanted to say more but she turned and walked out, glancing quickly over her shoulder with a grin before rushing downstairs and throwing on her bikini as she grabbed her phone and texted her best friend.

April wasn't entirely sure what had just happened, but she knew she loved it. And she knew she loved it with Ben.

He was the first real man she'd ever had like that. And she wanted more. Much, much more.

The only question was: Did he?

4

Shower Time

Ben couldn't stop himself when he saw April in that tiny bikini, standing there, wanting him.

For a split second, he thought about just going back to work, so he snapped at her about her social media. But when he saw the hurt look in her eyes and she called him an asshole he knew he'd gone too far. As soon as he had her in his arms, he wanted her, too.

She had tasted salty and sweet, her pussy so perfectly groomed he couldn't stop tasting her until she came all over his mouth. When he looked up at her after, he'd seen a trust and an excitement on her face that made him stop there. And then she had disappeared and never

come back that day. Now it was the
next day, and almost time for him
to leave and he still hadn't seen her.
He shook his head as he cleaned
up. He was almost done. Another
day and he'd be gone.

"Hey."

He turned at her voice and
immediately smiled. She was
wearing a short blue dress that was
a corset up top and a cute little skirt
at the bottom. Her hair was swept
into a cute ponytail and her make-
up was done perfectly.

"Wow," he said. "You
look…stunning."

"I want you to stay for dinner,"
she said quietly. "I mean, if you
don't have plans."

He grinned. "I don't have plans."

She tucked her hands behind her
back and swung them as she
smiled. Damn she was the cutest
thing he'd ever seen.

"I'd like to run home and take a shower, though, if that's okay? Be back in like twenty?"

She shook her head as a wicked little smile crossed her face. Without saying a word, she unzipped her dress and let it fall off her body onto the floor.

"Oh my God," he breathed. She was wearing nothing underneath her dress, standing there naked and beautiful in her high heels. "April."

"You can shower here." She slowly walked to him and slid her hands under his T-shirt, helping him take it off. He pulled her to him, feeling her soft breasts against his chest. It was intoxicating as he slid his hands up her back and into her hair, taking her lips in his and deeply kissing her.

She slid her hands down his chest to his belt buckle and undid him, sliding his jeans and boxer briefs down his legs. She gasped

when her delicate hand found his
hard cock and realized its length.

He grinned at her as she stroked
him.

"Be gentle," she whispered.

"I promise," he said.

He stepped out of his boots and
clothes, picked her up as she
wrapped her legs around him, and
headed to the finished shower,
turning on the hot water. As it
steamed up, he stepped inside and
they found their way to the wall,
the water pounding his back.

"April," he moaned. He set her
down and rubbed her body as he
kissed down to her wet pussy and
dove in. He slid his fingers between
her legs thrusting as he licked her
slit. She grabbed his hair and this
time directed his tongue as she
started to squirm.

"Ben, yes!"

Before she could come he stood up and put her nipples in his mouth, one at a time, as she panted.

"Ben, yes!" She reached down and started to stroke his cock as he moaned. "Baby, fuck me, please."

"Whatever you want, baby," he said. He picked her up again as she spread her legs and wrapped them around his waist. He put his tip at her entrance and looked in her eyes. "I'll go slow."

She nodded with a smile as he started to enter her. He went slow and easy as she adjusted to his size.

"Oh, baby," she said gasping. "Holy shit."

"Tell me to stop any time, okay?"

She nodded as he gently kissed her.

"Don't stop," she panted. She pushed against him as his length went deeper and deeper. "Ben!"

He could see the pleasure on her face as he slowly sunk inside her, now all the way in.

"You okay?" he asked gently. She nodded as he started to move slowly inside her. "This feel good?"

"Yeah," she said softly. "More, baby."

He started to thrust a little harder. "Like this?"

She kissed him then as he thrust even deeper. A moan of pleasure erupted in her throat.

"Yes!" She gripped onto him and pulled him in as her hips thrust toward him, pulling him deeper inside her. "Harder!"

He let loose then. She was so tight and wet; he could hardly stand It. Already he could feel his orgasm building.

"April, you're so tight and wet, fuck," he moaned.

"Baby that feel so good," she yelled. "Harder!"

He thrust deep and then stayed there with little pulses as she moaned.

"I'm gonna come," she moaned. "Right there, baby."

He stayed there, pulsing on her G-spot as she writhed with pleasure.

"I'm coming!" He could feel her pussy tighten and spasm around his cock as she came hard and fast.

"Come, baby, yes," he ordered. He fucked her good like that until she relaxed from the pleasure, then he thrust into her hard and fast. "I'm gonna come."

He thrust until he felt his orgasm ready to explode, then pulled out and came all over her legs and pussy.

"Yes, baby, yes," she said. "Come all over me."

"Fuck," he moaned. It was more come than he'd ever seen. He couldn't help it. April brought it out in him. He slowly put her down and rinsed her and himself off in the hot, steaming water as he quickly washed off.

"This feels a little late," he said as he grinned at her. "But, can I buy you dinner?"

She laughed and it was the sweetest thing he'd heard in a long time.

"I'd love to," she said.

"Cool," he said. He shut off the water. "Shall we?"

As they stepped out of the shower, she grabbed her clothes and walked into the bedroom. He grabbed his and followed. Everything he thought about April was turning out to be wrong. He was going to take the next two days to really get to know her and see if there was anything there.

And he secretly hoped that there
was.

5

More Than a Pretty Face

It was his last day on the job, and he'd done as he promised himself. He took the time to get to know April. He now knew she was elf-made, that she bought this place on her own, that she was standing on her own two feet and had since she was eighteen. She was, by any account, impressive.

He was interested now in seeing if this thing had legs to be something more. As much as he admired her and loved the sex they were having, they were still two very different people in how they lived and approached life.

In the past, he would look at someone like April, who wasn't like what he thought he wanted, and tell them it was just about the sex and walk away when it had run its course.

He wasn't sure where April fit in that mold. She definitely wasn't what he thought was someone he could be serious about—she wasn't someone he'd pictured. She was spoiled and a little superficial. Plus, he was pretty sure her father would hate him.

But he liked her. He liked her a lot. She was fun, and she made him more fun in turn. She was open and sweet and honest, and she had made it on her own. It made him think that, maybe, just this once, he should lighten up and let it happen.

He'd decide before he left. They were having dinner after he was done. She was ordering Chinese and renting something on Prime.

There was also the issue of whether he was *her* type. He wasn't like anyone she'd dated in her world before she left. And since then, it'd been party guys in college and that was it. In her words, he was the first "real man" she'd been with. And blue collar at that. Plus, he was military, and he knew he could be a strict, scheduled pain in the ass. Did she want to try with him?

"So, you want Pad Thai, extra spicy?" she asked as she popped her head into the bathroom. "Oh my God."

She walked in with her eyes wide open. "Ben, this is gorgeous."

"Makes a difference once it's all cleaned up and put together, doesn't it?"

"Totally," she said. She looked at him. "Thank you. Really, thank you for making it perfect."

Her eyes were so sincere when she looked at him, it melted his heart. Maybe there was something here.

"You're welcome, April," he whispered.

"I'll order this food if you wanna grab a shower."

"Okay," he said.

As she sashayed out, he turned on the shower and hopped in. It took only a few minutes to wash off and clean up. He hopped out and picked up his dirty clothes. He'd brought an overnight bag and left it in the bedroom. When he walked in, he had to catch his breath.

"April," he said quietly.

She had lit candles throughout the bedroom and was lying on the bed completely naked, her hair falling around her kind smile.

"Food will be here in an hour," she said. She smiled. "I thought we could keep ourselves busy until then."

He dropped his clothes and walked to her bed, sliding next to her, and pulling her into his arms. He kissed her gently as she let out a little moan.

"April?"

"Yeah?"

He looked in her eyes. Yeah, he wanted to do this.

"How would you feel about seeing each other more? Like, outside of me being the help."

He cracked a grin at her as she laughed.

"You know I only said that to get under your skin," she said.

"I do." They shared a sweet smile.

"I'd love to see you outside of this. Get to know each other even more, yes."

He felt a rush of relief and happiness as she kissed him, then trailed down his neck to his chest.

"Yes," he whispered. She rolled him onto his back and kissed down to his pelvis, landing her soft lips on his hard cock. "Oh God."

She took the tip of his cock into her mouth and licked the pre-come off it as she gently and slowly took him into her mouth.

"April, fuck," he moaned. She took him deeper and deeper, using one hand to grip and stroke his base and the other to gently cup his balls. He started to move his hips in time with her mouth, sliding his hand in her hair. It felt so fucking good. "Baby, stop, or I'll come."

She released him from her grip as she kissed back up his chest and slid her wet pussy to his stiffness and positioning herself over it.

"I wanna ride you, baby," she purred.

"Baby, yes," he moaned. The feeling of her tight, slick wetness gently pulling him inside of her was amazing. When she slid all the way down on his manhood, he nearly came. "Fuck, April!"

"You like that, baby?" She started riding his cock, slow and sensual, then quick and hard, rotating the pressure and driving him crazy. He grabbed her hips and slapped her ass. "Fuck, yes, baby, again!"

He gave her another slap on the ass spurring her on as she rode his cock, banging his balls with her sweet little ass.

"April, fuck, I'm gonna come," he yelled.

"Yes, baby, come!" she panted. "Come inside me."

"Yes!" he moaned as he came hard and fast, pulling her hips closer so he bury himself deep inside her.

"I'm coming," she moaned. He could feel her pussy grip him as she came hard.

As they both slowed down while their orgasms washed over them, Ben grinned at her and put his hands in her hair. He pulled her down to him as he kissed her, then pulled her to the side and curled up next to her.

"You're amazing, April," he said.

"You, too," she whispered. "I can't wait to learn more."

"Me, too," he said.

And he knew he meant every word of it.

6

Business or Pleasure?

Ben waited for the guys to respond as he grinned at them.

"Wow," Wolfe said. "Hey, if she makes you happy, that's all that matters."

"Agreed," said Jack. "If you get along, who cares if she fits some picture you had in your head?"

"It's actually kind of like me with Jenny," Danny said. He shrugged. "She's not like anything I would have ever thought I'd like. And we've been talking for a few months now. You never know."

Ben nodded at his buddies. "So, you don't think we're too different?"

"Do you?" Wolfe asked.

"I'm still deciding," Ben said. "But I think…I don't think it's a big deal. Not like I thought."

They all grinned at him.

"Alright, assholes, you're right," Ben relented.

"There it is," Jack said.

"I follow your girl already," Wolfe said. They all looked at him. "Smoothies. They're fuckin' killer, man."

"Yeah, you try the banana-rama one?" Danny asked.

"So good," Wolfe agreed.

"The power greenie is the winner," Ben said. "That damn thing gives me energy all morning."

"Sounds like you need it, all that sex you're having," Jack said.

They all laughed.

"You know it," Ben said.

"Alright, alright, we need to meet this girl now," Wolfe said. "Party at my new place in a month

when I actually sign the lease and
get a move-in date."

"You'll get to see the reno I did.
It's a beauty," Danny said.

"Sweet." Wolfe nodded.

"In the meantime, the next
renovation is up. Wolfe, you got
that one?" Danny asked.

Wolfe nodded. "I do."

"Business or pleasure?" Jack
asked.

Wolfe smiled. "I guess we'll see.

Ben and April's sexy story isn't over! Keep reading the *Men Who Renovate Erotic Series* to see what happens to him and his sexy friends! Wanna learn more about the other men—Danny, Jack, and Wolfe? Keep reading the *Men Who Renovate Erotic Series* as they build their business, enjoy sex, and talk about it all!

Scan me

<u>**Review this book!**</u>

Do you love *April Showers* as part
of the *Men Who Renovate Erotic
Series*? Then tell everyone about it!
Leave a review on Amazon.com!

Scan me